FRANCE

LETTERS FROM AROUND THE WORLD

Teresa Fisher

Photographs by Andy Johnstone

CHERRYTREE BOOKS

LETTERS FROM AROUND THE WORLD

Distributed in the United States by
Cherrytree Books
1980 Lookout Drive
North Mankato, MN 56001

Library of Congress Cataloging-in-Publication Data
Fisher, Teresa
    France / Teresa Fisher
      p.cm. -- (Letters from around the world)
    First published: London: Evans Brothers, 2003
    Includes bibliographical references and index.
    ISBN 1-84234-250-9 (alk. paper)
    1. France--Juvenile literature. 2. France--Social life and
customs--Juvenile literature. 3. Children--France--Social
life and customs--Juvenile literature. 4. Children--France
--Correspondence--Juvenile literature.
    I. Title. II. Series.

DC33.7.F5 2004 2005
44--dc29
                                        2004041444

First Edition
9 8 7 6 5 4 3 2 1

First published in 2003 by
Evans Brothers Ltd
2A Portman Mansions
Chiltern Street
London W1U 6NR

Conceived and produced by

Nutshell
MEDIA

www.nutshellmedialtd.co.uk

Editor: Polly Goodman
Design: Mayer Media Ltd
Cartography: Encompass Graphics Ltd
Artwork: Mayer Media Ltd
Consultants: Jeff Stanfield and Anne Spiring

Picture acknowledgments
All photographs were taken by Andy Johnstone
except: p26 (bottom) Britstock (Yashiro Haga);
p28 (Eiffel Tower) Dorian Shaw.

Printed in China.

Acknowledgments
The photographer would like to thank Yvonne, Patrick,
Victor and Germain Calsou, and the staff of Jules Julien
School, Toulouse, for all their help with this book.

Cover: Victor and friends in front of the River Garonne.
Title Page: Victor in the school playground.
This page: The peaks of the Pyrenees mountains.
Contents page: Victor carrying a freshly baked baguette
home for breakfast.
Glossary page: Victor reads a favorite book, *The Magic
Spuds*, in his bedroom.
Further Information page: People dressed up for the Mardi
Gras celebrations in Toulouse.
Index: One of the many bridges over the River Garonne.

Contents

My Country

Wednesday, January 9

46 Avenue des Avions
42703 Toulouse
France

Dear Jo,

Bonjour! (You say "bonj-or". This means "hello" in French.)

My name's Victor Calsou. I'm 9 years old. I live in Toulouse, a big city in the south of France. Look on the map to find Toulouse. I've got an older brother named Germain, who's 10.

It's great to be your pen pal. I'll be able to help you with class projects on France.

Write back soon!

From

Victor

This is my family on a bike ride. I'm the one in the middle. Do you have a bike?

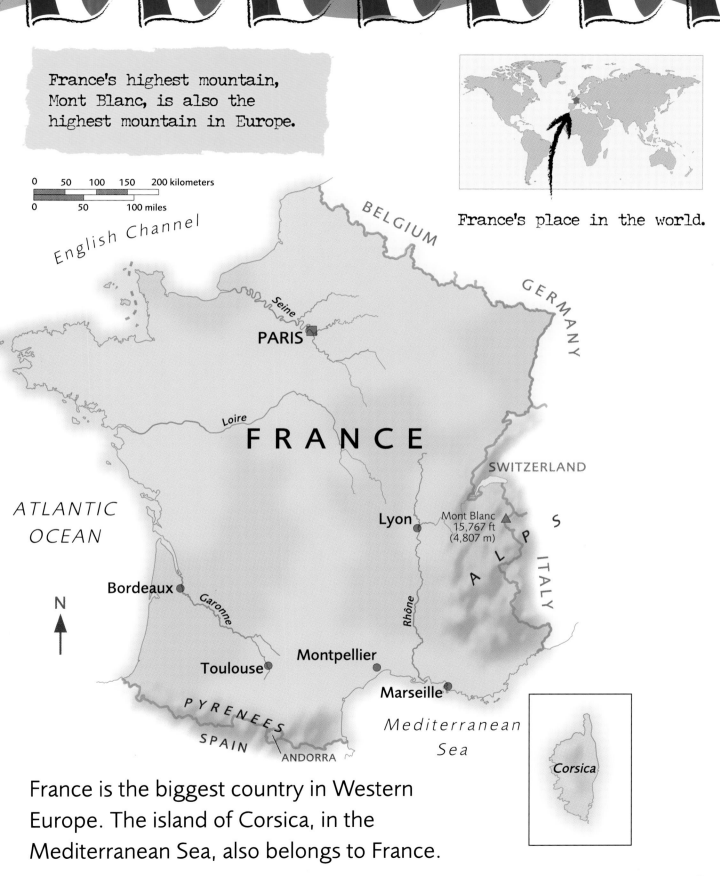

France's highest mountain, Mont Blanc, is also the highest mountain in Europe.

France's place in the world.

0   50   100   150   200 kilometers
0   50   100 miles

English Channel

BELGIUM

GERMANY

Seine

PARIS

Loire

F R A N C E

SWITZERLAND

ATLANTIC OCEAN

Lyon

Mont Blanc
15,767 ft
(4,807 m)

A L P S

ITALY

Rhône

N

Bordeaux

Garonne

Toulouse

Montpellier

Marseille

P Y R E N E E S

SPAIN

ANDORRA

Mediterranean Sea

Corsica

France is the biggest country in Western Europe. The island of Corsica, in the Mediterranean Sea, also belongs to France.

Most people in France live in big towns and cities near the coast or, like Toulouse, by a river. Toulouse is the fourth-largest city in France. More than half a million people live there.

The city is famous for making aircraft and space rockets. Toulouse University is the second-biggest university in France after Paris.

The Garonne River flows through the center of Toulouse.

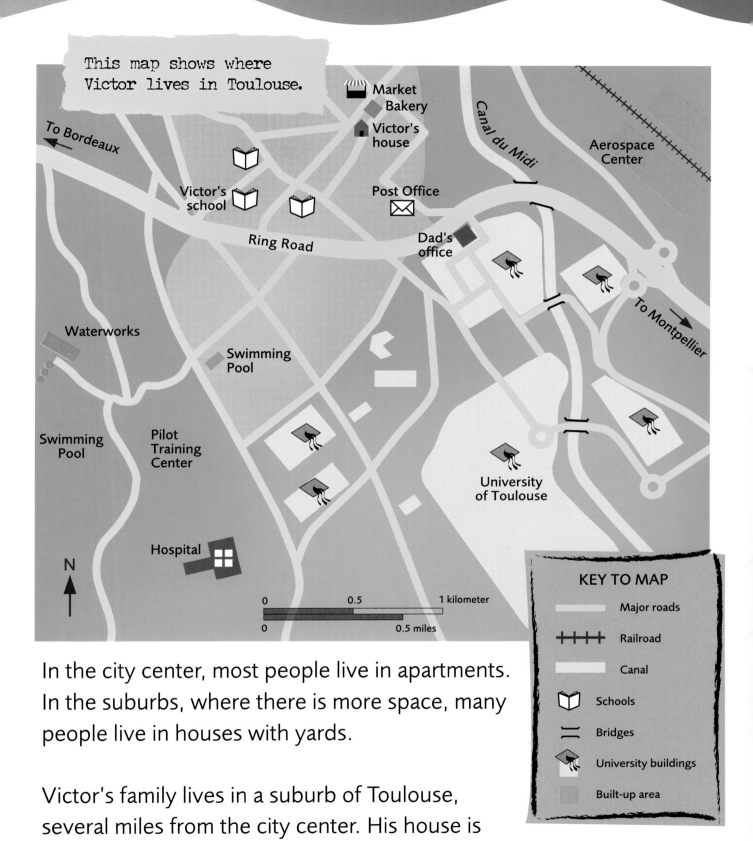

This map shows where Victor lives in Toulouse.

Market
Bakery
Victor's house
Canal du Midi
Aerospace Center
To Bordeaux
Victor's school
Post Office
Dad's office
Ring Road
To Montpellier
Waterworks
Swimming Pool
Swimming Pool
Pilot Training Center
University of Toulouse
Hospital
N

| 0 | 0.5 | 1 kilometer |
| 0 | | 0.5 miles |

KEY TO MAP

Major roads

Railroad

Canal

Schools

Bridges

University buildings

Built-up area

In the city center, most people live in apartments. In the suburbs, where there is more space, many people live in houses with yards.

Victor's family lives in a suburb of Toulouse, several miles from the city center. His house is near the university where his dad works.

Landscape and Weather

Toulouse is surrounded by rolling farmland and vineyards. To the south are the Pyrenees mountains. To the southeast, the sandy beaches of the Mediterranean Sea are just two hours away by car.

The Pyrenees are covered by snow in the winter. People go there to ski.

The climate in the south of France is hotter and drier than in the north. Summers in Toulouse are long and dry — ideal for growing grapes.

Toulouse's Climate

January	July
Temperature	**Temperature**
45 °F (7 °C)	73 °F (23 °C)
Rainfall 2–3 in (65 mm)	**Rainfall** 1–2 in (45 mm)

Flowers grow well in Toulouse's hot summer climate. Sunflower seeds are used to make sunflower oil.

At Home

Victor's family lives in a traditional-style house with a small yard. The windows have wooden shutters, which are closed in the summer to keep the house cool. They are also shut at night.

Victor and his family outside their house, with their cat, Saphir. *Saphir* is French for "Sapphire."

On the ground floor there is a large living room, where the family watches television and listens to the radio. They have a separate dining room and a kitchen.

Upstairs there is a bathroom and three bedrooms. There is also a study, where Victor's dad sometimes works on the computer.

The Calsou family has seven television channels to choose from.

Victor does his homework in his bedroom and reads his favorite books there.

Victor often helps his mom in the kitchen. One of his jobs is to load the dishwasher.

Victor and Germain have to help with the housework and keep their bedrooms tidy. Sometimes they help do the gardening, or wash the family's two cars. But it is much more fun playing with their toys.

Victor and Germain love playing with building sets.

Thursday, March 14

46 Avenue des Avions
42703 Toulouse
France

Bonjour Jo!

Thanks for your letter last week. Did I tell you that it was Germain's birthday yesterday? He was 11. After school, his best friend Etienne came over. Mom made a delicious almond cake. It's our favorite!

Then we played with Germain's presents. He got a new bicycle from Mom and Dad. I gave him some marbles. When's your birthday? Write back and tell me — mine's in May.

From
Victor

Germain always tries to get the biggest piece of cake!

Food and Mealtimes

On school days Victor wakes up at 7 a.m. For breakfast he has hot chocolate and croissants, or crusty bread with jam. Sometimes he has cereal with milk. There is always bread with every meal. The bread is usually long, thin loaves, called baguettes.

Every morning, Victor and Germain buy fresh baguettes and croissants from the local bakery.

The main meal of the day is usually the evening dinner, which all the family eats together. Often there are four courses — appetizers, a meat or fish dish with vegetables, then cheese, followed by dessert.

Victor drinks his hot chocolate from a bowl, which is the custom in France.

Victor loves food, especially cheese, pâté, and oysters, which are typical French dishes. One French dish that he does not like is snails with garlic butter, but his mom and dad think they are delicious.

Sunday, May 5

46 Avenue des Avions
42703 Toulouse
France

Hi Jo,

Thanks for the recipe you sent last week. Here's one for you.
It's for my favorite dessert — crêpes.

You will need: 2 cups flour, a little salt, 2 eggs, 2 cups milk,
3 tablespoons melted butter, jam, or sugar and lemon juice.

1. Add the eggs, milk, melted butter, and salt slowly to the flour and
   whisk everything together until it's smooth. Leave for one hour.
2. Pour a little of the mixture into a hot, greased frying pan and cook
   quickly over a high heat until the bottom of the crêpe is golden.
   (Mom always does that part for me.)
3. Flip the crêpe over, cook the other side and put it on a plate.
4. Spread a little jam, or sugar and lemon juice, on to the crêpe.
   Roll it up and serve immediately.

I hope you like them!

From
Victor

Here I am breaking
the eggs.

School Day

Victor and Germain go to the local primary
school, just ten minutes' walk from their home.
If it is raining, their dad takes them in his car.
Like most French schoolchildren, they
do not wear a school uniform.

Victor and Germain
always cross at the
pedestrian crossing on
their way to school.

Victor uses a writing board in math class. The board can be wiped clean for new work.

Lessons start at 8:30 a.m. and end at 4:30 p.m, with a two-hour lunch-break in the middle of the day.

There are 25 children in Victor's class. They study French, English, math, geography, history, and science, all with the same class teacher.

Victor has lunch every day in the cafeteria. Some of his friends go home for lunch.

During the lunch-break, Victor plays marbles in the school playground.

In France, children start school at the age of 6. Victor will stay at primary school until he is 11. Then he will go to secondary school. After that he hopes to go to college.

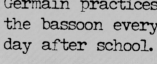

Germain practices the bassoon every day after school.

Friday July 19

46 Avenue des Avions
42703 Toulouse
France

Bonjour Jo!

I'm glad you liked the crêpes. I prefer them with jam, too.

Did I tell you that in France we don't have classwork on Wednesday afternoons? It gives us time to do other things like sports, painting, music, or drama at the local youth club.

My favorite sport's soccer. I also like wood carving. I go to a wood-carving club every Wednesday. Germain belongs to a rugby club. Do you belong to any clubs or teams?

From

Victor

These are some of Germain's friends playing rugby in their after-school club.

Off to Work

Victor's dad is a biology researcher at Toulouse University. His mom helps local schools to plan their lessons. Both parents start work at 8:30 a.m. They travel to work in their cars.

Victor's dad is doing an experiment in the laboratory.

There are lots of different types of work in Toulouse. Some people work in banks, stores or companies. Others work in factories. Outside the city, farmers grow crops and raise animals.

This man is a goat farmer. He uses goat's milk to make delicious cheeses.

23

Free Time

Victor spends his free time drawing, painting, reading, playing with his toys, and watching television. He loves playing soccer with his friends, going to the movies, or swimming at the local pool.

Everyone enjoys meeting friends in cafés in France.

On weekends, Victor often goes on a bike ride with his family. During vacations, they go hiking in the Pyrenees mountains. Sometimes they visit England.

Victor's brother plays with a juggling toy, called a diabolo. He throws it in the air and then catches it on the string.

The bike path along the river is great for bike rides.

Religion and Festivals

These children are dressed up for a local festival in southwest France.

Most people in France are Roman Catholic, but there are other religions, too, including Islam and Judaism.

Christmas and Easter are the most important Roman Catholic festivals. Forty days before Easter, there is an exciting carnival called Mardi Gras in Toulouse.

At Mardi Gras, everyone dresses up for a big nighttime procession.

Monday, December 23

46 Avenue des Avions
42703 Toulouse
France

Hi Jo,

I'm really excited because tomorrow it's Christmas Eve. Do you celebrate Christmas, too?

I've been decorating the house with tinsel. Tomorrow we'll have a big meal with my grandparents and give out presents. I'm hoping for a new bike. Then we'll go to church for a special service at midnight. It's great being awake at midnight.

Joyeux Noël! (This means "Merry Christmas" in French.)

From

Victor

This is me decorating the Christmas tree. It's not a real tree, so we can use it again every year.

Fact File

Capital City: Paris. The city has many famous museums, art galleries, and buildings, including the Eiffel Tower. Visitors can take an elevator to the top or they can climb the 1,652 steps! On a clear day you can see for up to 40 miles (70 km) from the top of the tower.

Language: French is the official language of France and of another 21 countries in the world.

Flag: The French flag is called the *tricolore*, which means "three-colored." Red and blue represent the city of Paris and white is the traditional color for French kings.

Highest mountain: Mont Blanc, 15,767 feet (4,807 m). This is in the Alps, in southeast France.

Longest River: The Loire, 630 miles (1,020 km). It flows from the middle of France to the Atlantic Ocean.

Famous Products: France is famous for its cars, aircraft, and perfume, and for its fashions, fine cooking, and wines. The most famous wine is a fizzy white wine called champagne.

Fastest Trains: French trains (called TGV) are the fastest in the world. They reach speeds of up to 200 mph (300 kph).

Currency: The euro (€). This replaced French francs in January 2002. It is the currency used by 12 out of the 25 member countries of the European Union.

Festivals: There are more than 400 festivals in France. The biggest is called Bastille Day, on July 14. Many are religious festivals, such as Purim (above), Christmas, and Easter.

Tourism: More people visit France for their vacations than any other country in Europe. One of the biggest attractions for children is Disneyland, in Paris.

Stamps: Most French stamps are fairly plain, but sometimes they have pictures or cartoons on them.

Famous People:
Napoleon Bonaparte was an army general who became Emperor of France in 1804. Claude Monet (born in 1840) was a painter who led the Impressionist movement. Charles Perrault (born in 1628) wrote the fairy tales *Sleeping Beauty*, *Little Red Riding Hood,* and *Cinderella*.

Glossary

apartment A group of rooms to live in.

baguettes (You say "bag-et") Crusty bread, shaped like sticks.

bonjour! This means "hello" or "good day" in French.

carnival A big festival with music and dancing.

Christmas The birthday of Jesus Christ.

crêpes (You say "crep") Thin, round pancakes, served with either a sweet or a savory filling.

croissants (You say "kwa-son") A rich, buttery pastry shaped like a half-moon, often eaten at breakfast.

Easter A Christian festival when people remember Jesus rising from the dead.

European Union A group of 25 countries in Europe that work and trade together.

Joyeux Noël! This means "Merry Christmas" in French.

pâté (You say "pattay") A tasty meat paste, usually eaten with bread.

researcher Someone who makes careful investigations to find out new facts.

Roman Catholic A member of the Roman Catholic Church, the largest branch of Christianity. The head of this church is the Pope.

saint A title given to holy people by some Christian churches.

shutters Wooden, slatted doors attached to the outside of glass windows. They help keep houses cool in hot climates.

suburb A small district at the edge of a town or city.

Further Information

Information books:

Alcraft, Rob. *A Visit to France*. Chicago: Heinemann, 1999.

Boast, Claire. *Step into France*. Chicago: Heinemann, 1998.

Fisher, Teresa. *A Flavour of France*. London: Hodder & Stoughton, 1998.

Fisher, Teresa. *Country Insights: France*. Chicago: Raintree/Steck-Vaughn, 1997.

Fisher, Teresa. *We Come from France*. London: Hodder & Stoughton Childrens Division, 2001.

Phillips, Charles. *Fiesta! France*. Danbury, CT: Grolier, 1999.

Pluckrose, Henry. *Picture a Country: France*. London: Franklin Watts, 1999.

Townsend, Sue. *A World of Recipes: France*. Chicago: Heinemann, 2002.

Fiction:

Anholt, Laurence. *Degas and the Little Dancer, A story of Edgar Degas*. Barrons Juveniles, 1996.

St Exupéry, Antoine de. *The Little Prince*. Harcourt, 2000.

Resource Packs:

Un, Deux, Trois: First French Rhymes (Frances Lincoln, 2003)
A selection of French nursery rhymes for young children, including an audio-cassette.

Web sites:

CIA Factbook
www.cia.gov/cia/publications/factbook/
Basic facts and figures about France and other countries.

French Tourist Office
www.franceguide.com/

Index